What Can a Baby Do?

Sarah Churchill
Charles Fuge

GULLANE
CHILDREN'S BOOKS

Hello! My name is
Ollie.
Do you know
what I can do?

Turn the pages of
this book – it might
give you a clue . . .

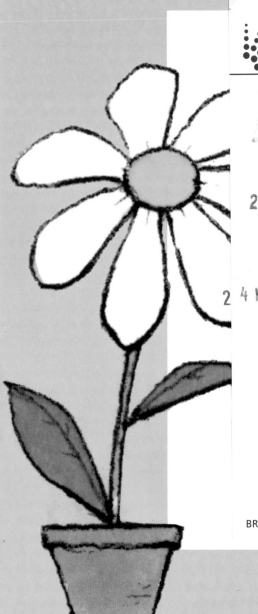

For Oliver

First published in Great Britain in 2008 by Gullane Children's Books.
This paperback edition published in 2009 by

Gullane Children's Books

185 Fleet Street, London EC4A 2HS

1   3   5   7   9   10   8   6   4   2

Text © Sarah Churchill & Charles Fuge 2008
Illustrations © Charles Fuge 2008

ISBN: 978-1-86233-751-0

Printed and bound in Indonesia

Can I
grow a flower
and water it each day?

Can I
drive a tractor
through fields
of golden hay?

Can I
charm a snake
with music soft
and sweet?

Can I
play the drums
and keep
a steady beat?

Can I
make a cake
and bake it
nice and hot?

Can I climb a mountain till I reach the very top?

Can I
hold on tight
and swing
between the trees?

Can I
sail a boat
across the
seven seas?

No!
I'm still a baby.

But one day
when I'm grown,
I'll climb
and cook
and sail . . .

and drive a tractor of my own.